CHARLIE CHOOSES

Lou Peacock

Nicola Slater

For Rafe, and for Charlie,
who always chooses.
Much love, L.P. xx

I dedicate this book to Leo . . .
actually make that to Finn.
No, Leo. No! Finn.
To Leo *and* Finn.
~ N.S.

First published 2021 by Nosy Crow Ltd
The Crow's Nest, 14 Baden Place, Crosby Row
London SE1 1YW
www.nosycrow.com

ISBN 978 1 78800 562 3 (HB)
ISBN 978 1 78800 563 0 (PB)

Nosy Crow and associated logos are trademarks and/or registered
trademarks of Nosy Crow Ltd
Text by Lou Peacock
Text © Nosy Crow 2021
Illustrations © Nicola Slater 2021

The right of Lou Peacock to be identified as the author and Nicola Slater
to be identified as the illustrator of this work has been asserted.

A CIP catalogue record for this book is available from the British Library.

Printed in China

1 3 5 7 9 8 6 4 2 (HB)
1 3 5 7 9 8 6 4 2 (PB)

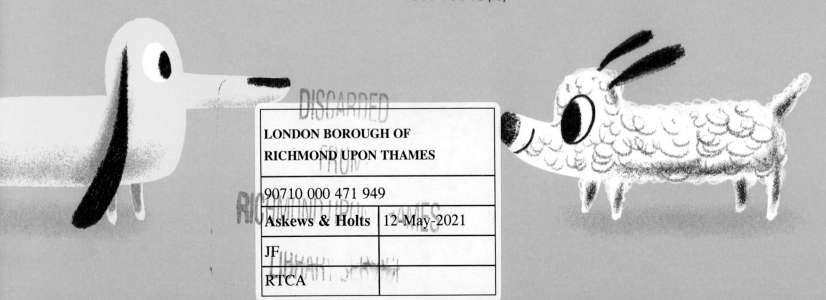

CHARLIE CHOOSES

Lou Peacock

Nicola Slater

Charlie did **not**
like to choose.

He never knew what was best . . .

. . . and Charlie always worried
that he might choose . . .

ICES

He could never choose between chocolate ice cream and vanilla ice cream, which sometimes meant that he had . . .

no ice cream at all.

He couldn't choose between
spotty pants and stripy pants,
and so he often did the simplest thing . . .

and wore **no pants** at all.

And bedtime was **never** easy.

Light off.

Light on.

Light off.

Light on.

"I can't choose!"
said Charlie.
"It's too hard!"

So sometimes he got
no sleep at all.

Poor Charlie. He knew he would **never** be able to choose a present for his birthday, so he did a very sensible thing and looked in a book.

The book was **full** of ideas . . .

a banana, a racing car, a top hat, a hot dog,
a firefighter outfit, an ant farm, a teddy bear, a guitar,
a bucket, a wobbly jelly, a button, a pair of socks . . .

but . . .

"I can't choose!"
said Charlie.

"It's too hard!"

And he went to have
a sit down.

When suddenly . . .

he had an idea.

"That's it!" said Charlie.

"A dog! A dog is
the **perfect** present."

And off he went to the rescue centre.

The rescue centre was **full** of dogs.

There were
small dogs

and tall dogs.

Fluffy dogs
and scruffy dogs.

White dogs
and black dogs.

Soppy dogs and floppy dogs.

Leapy dogs
and
sleepy dogs.

Long dogs and strong dogs.

Old dogs and bold dogs.

And every other kind of dog.

"I can't choose,"
whispered Charlie. "It's too hard."

He turned to go . . .

. . . but then something waggy and shaggy . . .

and mostly white, but a little bit brown . . .

scampered . . .

and jumped . . .

and dug a very, very big hole . . .

and ran and ran and ran . . .

. . . right into his arms!

"Oh!" said Charlie.

"I don't **have** to choose!
Because this dog . . .

has chosen **me**."

Now Charlie has someone who helps him
to choose ice cream . . .

and pick the
perfect pants.

And, when it's bedtime,
Charlie knows **exactly** what to do . . .

Light **off** . . .
and dog **on** the bed.

Now all Charlie has to do is choose a name . . .